The Days of Summer

WRITTEN BY **Eve Bunting**

ILLUSTRATED BY **William Low**

Harcourt, Inc.

San Diego   New York   London

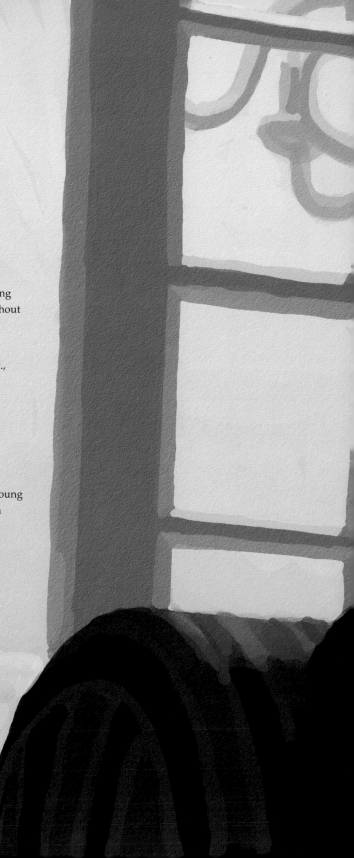

For Lael Littke and Gail Francis
—E. B.

Special thanks to Carly and Miranda
—W. L.

www.harcourt.com

Library of Congress Cataloging-in-Publication Data
Bunting, Eve, 1928–
The days of summer/by Eve Bunting; illustrated by William Low.
p. cm.
Summary: As summer ends and they get ready to go back to school, two young
girls try to deal with the news that the grandparents they love are getting a
divorce.
[1. Grandparents—Fiction.   2. Sisters—Fiction.   3. Divorce—Fiction.]
I. Low, William, ill. II. Title.
PZ7.B91527Dazk 2001
[E]—dc21   99-6822
ISBN 0-15-201840-9

First edition
H G F E D C B A

Printed in Hong Kong

The illustrations in this book were created using Photoshop.
The display type was set in Caxton Book.
The text type was set in Book Antiqua.
Printed by South China Printing Company, Ltd., Hong Kong
This book was printed on totally chlorine-free Nymolla Matte Art paper.
Production supervision by Sandra Grebenar and Pascha Gerlinger
Designed by Lori McThomas Buley

Grandma and Grandpa are getting a divorce.
Mom and Dad told us tonight. We can't believe it.

My little sister, Jo-Jo, and I lay in bed, talking.

"Grandma and Grandpa are really, really, really old," Jo-Jo said. "Really, really, really old people don't get divorced. Grandma and Grandpa are about a hundred."

"No they're not," I said. "They're sixty something. That's young for old people."

I could see Jo-Jo in the other bed. She was sitting up, hugging Carmen, our big black cat. Jo-Jo's five, and I think the cat's as big as she is.

She lay down. "Do they hate each other now?"

"Of course not. But sometimes I've heard them say things. They stop when they see I'm listening. They don't fight exactly. It's more as if they're not best friends anymore."

Carmen leaped with a thump from Jo-Jo's bed to mine, and Jo-Jo sat up again. Her voice was excited. "You know what, Nora? Molly and Whiffle got divorced. And then they got undivorced. Whiffle brought Molly a teddy bear in a pink dress with a petticoat that stuck out and—"

"Jo-Jo," I said, "Molly and Whiffle are in a cartoon."

We lay in silence awhile. Then Jo-Jo said, "Grandpa's so nice. And Grandma's teaching me dominoes."

Now she was crying. I got out of bed and cuddled in beside her. She's so skinny—skinny as the little starling that once flew against our window, and that I held for a minute before it fluttered away. I felt like bawling myself.

Even after Jo-Jo sobbed herself to sleep, I stayed warm beside her, watching the moon slide through the branches of the elm tree outside our window. Would we see both of them, or only one? After my friend Fiona's parents got divorced, she never saw her dad again. I couldn't bear it if we never saw Grandpa.

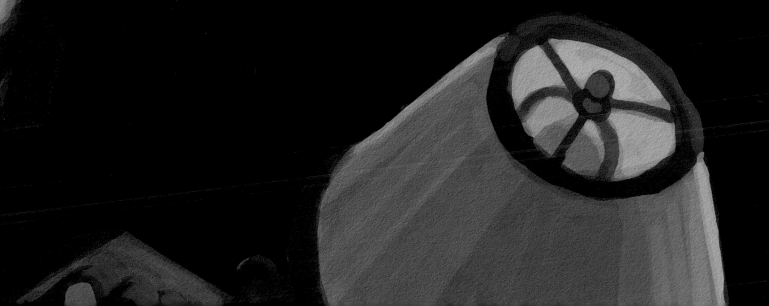

When we got up in the morning, Dad had already left for Compo-Computers, where he works. Mom was fixing French toast for breakfast instead of cereal. I guess it was to cheer us up. Or maybe because she had more time. She'd taken a week off work to get us ready for school. On Monday Jo-Jo's starting kindergarten and I'm starting fourth grade.

"Why couldn't Grandma and Grandpa just stay together?" I asked. "They've been together all this time."

"They've made a choice not to. We have to learn to deal with it." Mom sounded calm, but her hand shook as she slid my French toast onto my plate. Carmen was up on the counter, sniffing at the tomatoes in the bowl. Mom usually swats her when she tries a trick like that. Today she paid no attention.

Jo-Jo sat back in her chair. "I'm never going to eat again, until Grandma and Grandpa get undivorced," she announced.

"Sweetie, they're not divorced yet," Mom said. She came to sit at the table. "It takes time. But I'm afraid it is going to happen. So eat your toast before it gets cold."

"Molly and Whiffle got undivorced," Jo-Jo said.

"Jo-Jo," I said, "forget them. They're chipmunks."

Mom poured herself a cup of coffee. "Well," she said in a fake cheerful voice, "no matter what, life goes on. And we have a lot to do this week. You both have the dentist today. And Jo-Jo has to get new shoes."

"With bows," Jo-Jo said.

"No bows." Mom took out her list.

"Are we still going to Grandma and Grandpa's on Sunday?" I asked.

"Yes. But I'm afraid Grandpa won't be there. He has already moved out." Mom's coffee cup jiggled as she set it back in the saucer. "Oh, sweeties, I'm so sad about this. But I'm trying not to be gloomy, and I need you to help me."

I thought how bad it must be for her. These were her *parents*. I stroked her hair, and she smiled.

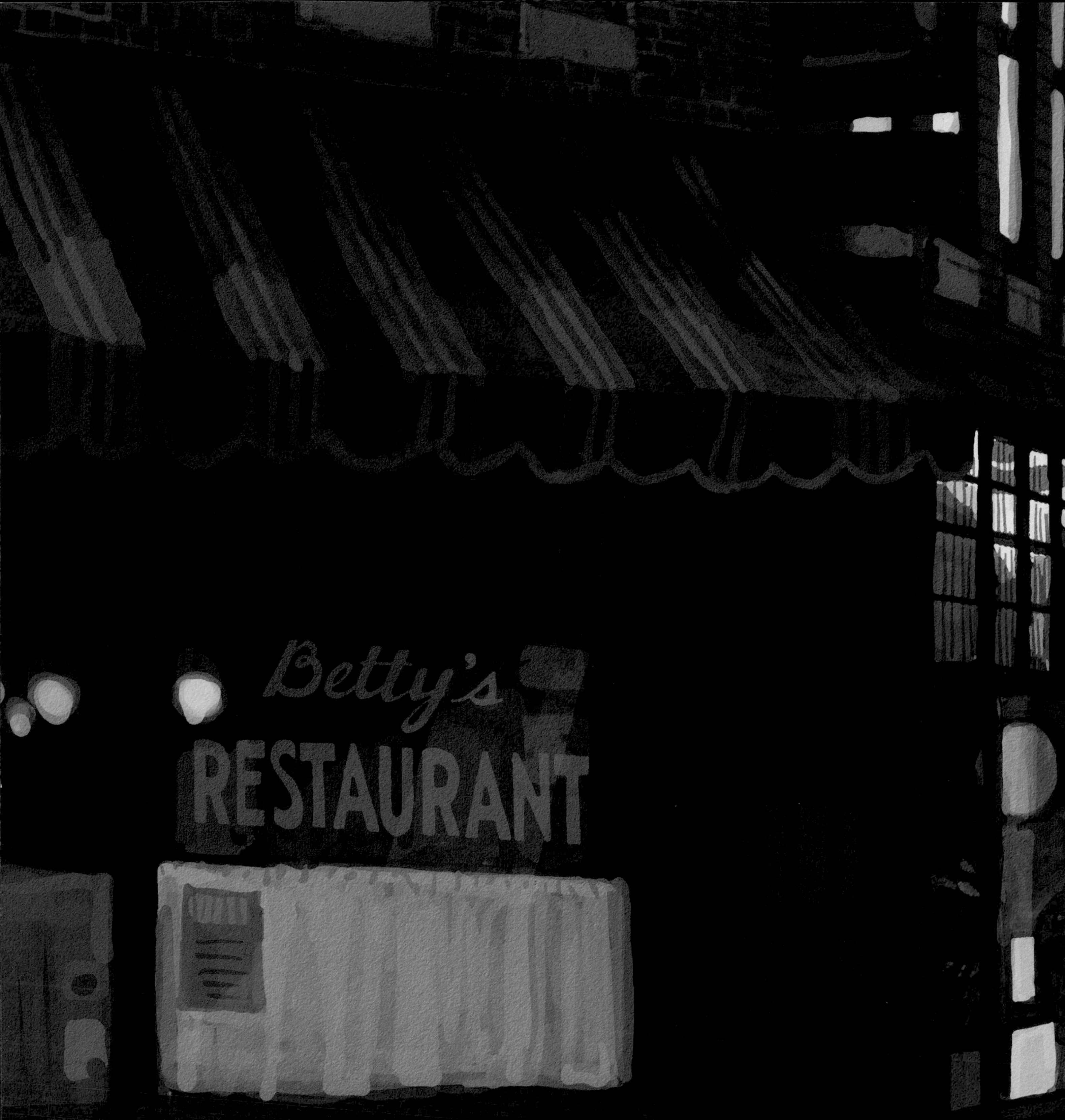
Betty's
RESTAURANT

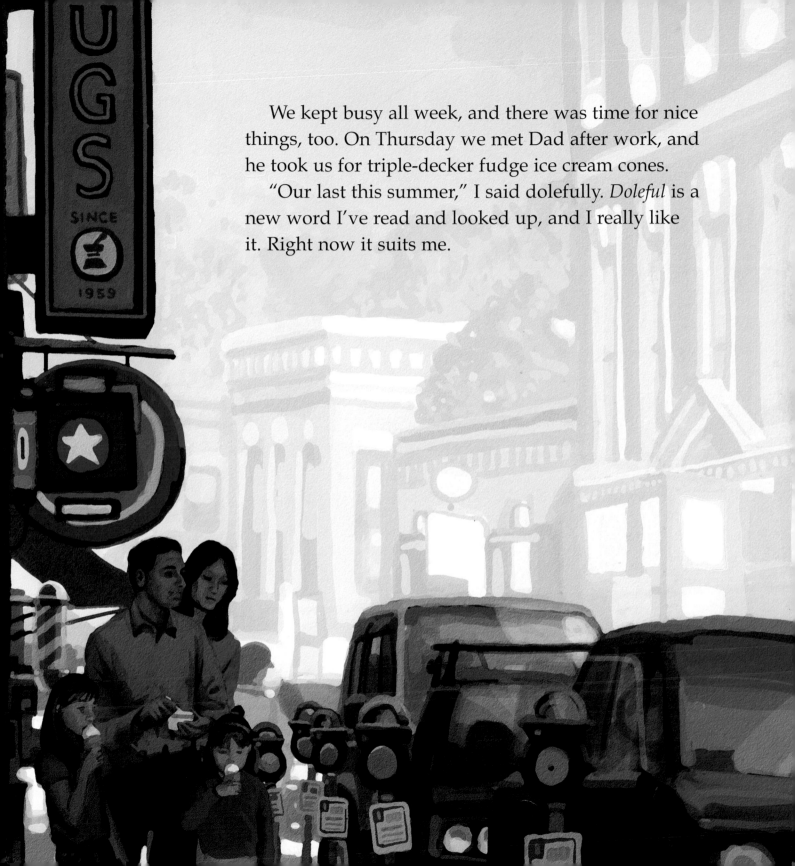

We kept busy all week, and there was time for nice things, too. On Thursday we met Dad after work, and he took us for triple-decker fudge ice cream cones.

"Our last this summer," I said dolefully. *Doleful* is a new word I've read and looked up, and I really like it. Right now it suits me.

On Friday the three of us rode bikes to the park and fed the ducks.
"Our last time to feed the ducks this summer," I said.

On Saturday night, when Dad and Mom were tucking me in,
I said, "The last time you'll let me read in bed till nine-thirty."
"There'll still be weekends," Mom said.

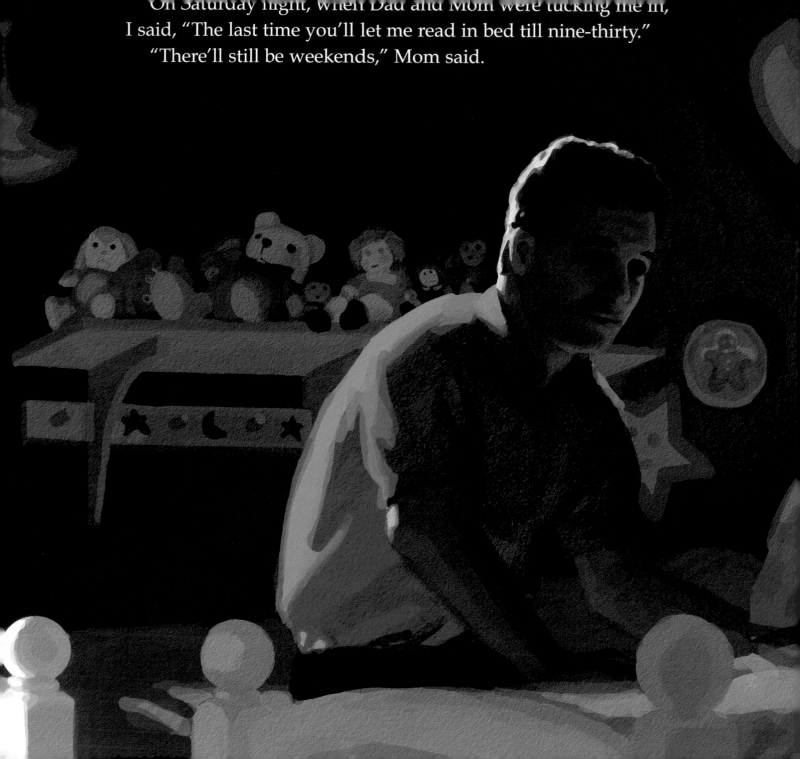

And then it was Sunday, and we were going to our grandparents' house for dinner.

"This is going to be very hard for Mom and Grandma," Dad told us as we were getting into our van. "Let's try our very best to deal with it, for them."

There were those words again, almost the same words Mom had said. They made me really doleful.

Grandma met us at the door. She seemed the same as ever.

"I'm sorry Grandpa's not here," she said right away. "He'll be coming over a lot for family dinners, though. Thanksgiving. Christmas." She was so ordinary about it. It was as if he had just gone on a trip.

Jo-Jo screwed up her face. "Please, please don't divorce Grandpa. I'll pay you not to. I've got thirty-three dollars. I'll give you every bit."

Grandma hugged us. "That's so generous of you, Jo-Jo. But I don't think it would help."

"It's so sad," I whispered.

Grandma kissed my cheek. "It *is* sad. But it's happy, too. Grandpa and I've known for a long time that this is what we should do. I guess it was just too hard a decision to make. And then, one day, we faced up to how unhappy we were together, and that time was passing. Weeks and months and years. Just the way the days of summer fly past for you, Nora. Suddenly it's time to go back to school and"—Grandma made a little face—"and suddenly it's all over. Grandpa and I will be better apart. Maybe we'll even be better friends." She spread her arms, and it was almost as if she were that starling, fluttering away to freedom. "Now, who'll help me get dinner on the table?"

"We will," Jo-Jo and I said together.

Grandma's dining table is big and round.
One of the chairs had been set back against the
wall, and I thought that was better than having
it empty at the table. It's ready for him when he
comes back, I thought.

We had peach pie for dessert. Peach pie
is Grandpa's favorite. I could hardly swallow.
The last peach pie of the summer, I thought.

When we'd helped with the dishes, Jo-Jo and I went out to the backyard to swing. Fireflies flickered around us as we swept up into the dark, trying to nudge the moon with our bare toes. I played a game with myself. If I trapped a firefly between my hands on my way up or down, there wouldn't be a divorce. But I didn't catch a single one.

Grandpa called later and talked to Jo-Jo and me on the two phones.

"We miss you so much," Jo-Jo whispered.

"And I miss you so much. But I want you to come next Saturday and see my new apartment. I'm not very far away. I'll never go far away from you. And guess what? The landlord says I can get a pet. Should I get a dog or a cat?"

"Both," we both said.

"Nothing's ever going to be the same again, is it?" I asked.

"No, sweetheart. Not the same."

We were quiet for a minute, then Grandpa said, "I don't expect you to understand, but maybe someday you will."

"It has to do with weeks and months and years passing," I said. "And doing things for the last time. And not wasting what's left."

"Oh, Nora!" Grandpa's voice was so loving that I wanted to cry.

When we'd said good-bye and hung up the phones, Jo-Jo said, "I was going to tell him about Molly and Whiffle. But I didn't think it would do any good."

As soon as we went
back in the living room, she
said, "Grandpa's getting
a dog *and* a cat."
"He's going to take us to see his new
apartment next Saturday," I said.
And then I noticed there was a piece of pie
left on the plate on the dining-room sideboard.
"Can I bring that for him?" I asked Grandma.
"Sure you can," she said. "I'll wrap it in foil.
Your mom can put it in the freezer till Saturday."
I held the pie gently all the way home. It was something
from us to him, something that joined us all together.
He wasn't very far away. He'd never go far away from us.
I'd learn to deal with it, I told myself.

And suddenly
I didn't feel quite so doleful.